GUNK ALIENS

THE NIT PICKER

Collect all the books in the *GUNK Aliens* series!

JONNY MOON

GUNK

ALIENS

THE NIT PICKER

HarperCollins *Children's Books*

First published in paperback in Great Britain by
HarperCollins *Children's Books* 2010
HarperCollins *Children's Books* is a division of HarperCollins*Publishers* Ltd
77-85 Fulham Palace Road, Hammersmith, London W6 8JB

The HarperCollins website address is:

www.harpercollins.co.uk

1

Copyright © HarperCollins 2010
Illustrations by Vincent Vigla
Illustrations © HarperCollins 2010

ISBN: 978-0-00-732617-4

Printed and bound in England by Clays Ltd, St Ives plc

Mixed Sources
Product group from well-managed
forests and other controlled sources
www.fsc.org Cert no. SW-COC-1806
© 1996 Forest Stewardship Council

FSC is a non-profit international organisation established to promote the
responsible management of the world's forests. Products carrying the FSC
label are independently certified to assure consumers that they come
from forests that are managed to meet the social, economic and
ecological needs of present and future generations.

Find out more about HarperCollins and the environment at
www.harpercollins.co.uk/green

Special thanks to Colin Brake,
GUNGE agent extraordinaire.

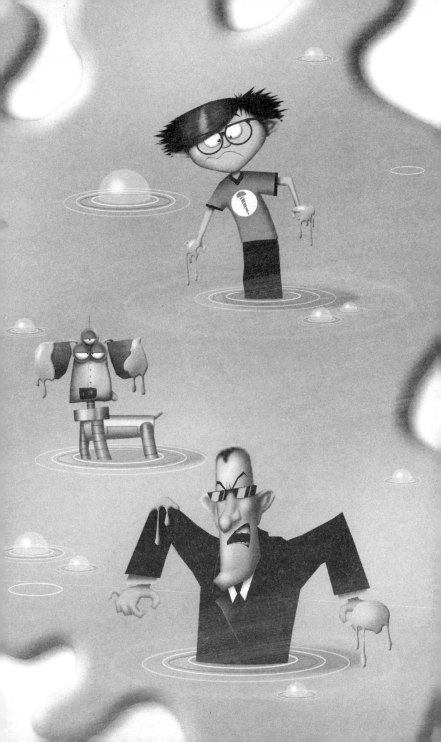

A long time ago, in a galaxy far, far away, a bunch of slimy aliens discovered the secret to clean, renewable energy...

... snot!

(Well, OK, clean-*ish*.)

There was just one problem. The best snot came from only one kind of creature.

Humans.

And humans were very rare. Within a few years, the aliens had used up all the best snot in their solar system.

That was when the Galactic Union of Nasty Killer Aliens (GUNK) was born. Its mission: to find human life and drain its snot. Rockets were sent to the four corners of the universe, each carrying representatives from the major alien races. Three of those rockets were never heard from again. But one of them landed on a planet quite simply *full* of humans.

This one.

CHAPTER ONE

"Right, this is it," announced Jack Brady in an excited whisper. His hand was trembling slightly as he reached out towards the new invention sitting on the workbench. In his hand he held the final component – the tiny data chip on to which he had loaded the voice command program.

Using tweezers, Jack carefully slipped the memory card into

position and then he closed the cover.

"Oscar, it's ready!" he announced.

Slipping his magnifying goggles from his face, Jack glanced over at his best friend Oscar, who was lounging on a beanbag and staring into space.

"Oscar!"

As if moving through treacle, Oscar slowly turned his head to look at Jack with half-asleep eyes. "Yeah?"

Jack peered at Oscar curiously. What was wrong with him? Jack was a thinker, a genius inventor who was always developing great new toys to play with, and Oscar, his best friend, was the man of action – Jack's first and most loyal crash-test dummy. Usually Oscar couldn't *wait* to have a go with whatever new invention Jack had come up with, but today he just didn't seem interested. It was like he was ill or something.

"It's a voice-recognition remote-control chopper," said Jack. "Don't you want to see what it can do?"

Oscar just shrugged. "Yeah, whatever. Maybe after school."

Jack sighed and looked over at his dog, Snivel. "Can you believe this, Snivel?"

Snivel shook his head. "No, but it is nearly time for you to go to school," he replied.

Snivel was not an ordinary dog. For a start he had three eyes.

"You need to keep that third eye of yours closed," Jack reminded him.

Snivel nodded and his face creased up with the effort, but finally he managed to close his third eye which was in the middle of his forehead. CLUNK! He fell over – the level of concentration causing him to lose his balance. Snivel was a robot dog. In fact, he

was a Snot-Bot. Powered by alien technology that used human snot as an energy source, Snivel's function was to assist Jack in locating and capturing aliens. Jack had been given Snivel by a secret organisation called GUNGE – the General Under-Committee for the Neutralisation of Gruesome Extraterrestrials – and together they had captured five aliens over the last few months.

Jack blew his nose, then checked his

tissue and tossed it over to his unusual dog.
"There you go," he said. "I've got a bit of a
cold again so you're in luck. Plenty of extra
treats for you!"

Gratefully Snivel sucked up the snot and
immediately bounced back on to his feet.
Jack picked up the now totally dry tissue
and put it back in his pocket. That snack
would keep Snivel's batteries powered for
the rest of the day. But he didn't think he'd
ever get used to the way the little robot
dog hoovered up his snot…

"You coming?" he said to Oscar as he
headed for the door of their tree house. But
the only reply he received was another
shrug of the shoulders. He stared at Oscar
who eventually let out a long, deep sigh.
He rose wearily to his feet and
followed Jack slowly down the
ladder.

The tree house which the boys shared was actually a large garden shed that Oscar's dad had won in a newspaper competition. The boys had houses that backed on to each other, and the large tree at the end of Oscar's garden was the perfect place for a tree house – so Oscar's dad had hired a crane to locate the shed safely in its branches.

Jack had been so keen to complete his latest invention that he had called Oscar over to the tree house early, before school, but now he was beginning to wonder why he had bothered. Oscar just didn't seem himself recently. As they walked to school, in unusual silence, Jack applied his genius brain to the problem. *What's wrong with Oscar?*

It didn't take Jack long to come up with an answer. It was obvious really. Oscar was clearly missing the excitement of their work with GUNGE fighting against the GUNK Aliens.

It had all started with a bin at the local park. Except it wasn't a bin, of course, it was really a pan-dimensional secret base from which the mysterious GUNGE agent named Bob had given instructions to Jack, Oscar and their friend Ruby. The base was bigger on the inside and able to move around to different hidden locations. The problem was that Bob had turned out to be a traitor and he had now stolen the base and moved it. The new Bob (who seemed to be a woman this time) had contacted the kids and given them a new mission. They had to locate the base – which was where the aliens they had caught were being held

– before any other members of the GUNK Alien alliance could find and rescue the captured aliens. Back in the summer holidays they had successfully managed to find it once, hidden in an off-shore wind farm, but before they could secure it, Bad Bob had managed to move the base again, leaving them back at square one. Since then there had been no contact from New Bob, and no sign of any alien activity. It had all gone very quiet. No wonder Oscar was a bit fed up.

Still not really talking, the boys reached Ruby's house. As usual Ruby was late. She had managed to get out of her front door, as she always did, but then, inevitably, she was held up by her over-protective mother.

"Have you got your vest on, darling?" Ruby's mother was saying as Jack and Oscar arrived at her driveway.

"Yes," hissed Ruby, who had seen her friends arriving and was now deeply embarrassed.

"And your inhaler?" asked Ruby's mum.

"Mum, I haven't had asthma since I was three," complained Ruby.

"Well, that's as may be, but you can't take any chances with something

like asthma," insisted her mother. "Especially with the change of weather."

Jack looked up at the sky, which was unblemished by a single cloud.

"It's been sunny for days,"

Ruby told her mum, narrowing her eyes.

Ruby's mum didn't miss a beat. "Exactly!" she said, thrusting her hand out and waving the asthma inhaler at Ruby. Ruby sighed, took the inhaler, dropped it into her school bag and hurried down the path to join her friends.

"And be careful when you cross that main road," called out Ruby's mother from her front door.

Jack couldn't help smiling as he saw Ruby roll her eyes in horror. "How old does she think you are?" he teased.

Ruby just shot him a dark look. "Don't!" she ordered him tersely.

Jack looked around and realised that Oscar was still standing at the end of Ruby's drive. Ruby turned to follow his gaze.

"Come on, Oscar, we're meant to be going to school, remember?" shouted Jack.

As if in a dream-world, Oscar turned his head towards the source of the words, a puzzled expression on his face. It was as if he had to think about each individual word that Jack had said before he could begin to answer.

Finally he seemed to be ready. "OK," he said and began to walk slowly towards them. Ruby and Jack headed for school.

"What's wrong with Oscar?" Ruby wondered.

Now it was Jack who was shrugging. "He's just in this weird mood," he confessed to Ruby. "He's been like that for days. Doesn't say much. Won't play with any of my inventions. Seems half asleep most of the time."

"He's not the only one," said Ruby.

"What do you mean?" said Jack.

"Other kids at school have been acting weird too. Haven't you noticed?"

Jack had to confess that he hadn't noticed anything of the sort.

"Well, that's no surprise," said Ruby laughing. "You're always in a dream world yourself."

"Not dreaming," said Jack, mock-seriously. "Thinking *very hard* about my inventions."

Ruby grinned. "Whatever. But the thing is,

loads of kids at school have been going around in a daze lately. Just like Oscar."

"Sort of like they're not all there?" said Jack.

Ruby nodded. "Exactly. And I can tell you exactly when it started too."

Jack looked at her expectantly.

"Ever since the new Nit Nurse came to school."

CHAPTER TWO

The Nit Nurse was a new thing for the school. Nits, however, were not. Ever since Jack had started school he'd regularly had to take a note home to his mum saying that 'someone' in his class had head lice and that she should take care to check Jack's hair and wash it with special anti-nit shampoo. Once Jack had even had nits himself! He would never forget the nightly nit hunt, with his mum scraping special liquid through his hair with a thin-toothed metal comb.

Jack's mum had told him that when she was young there had been a visitor in school who would check every child in every class for head lice. That was the proper name for nits – head lice. Jack thought it sounded really gross. Head lice were little insects that lived in children's hair and laid their eggs there too. People said that in some cases you could actually see the little creatures running around on kids' heads! There were all sorts of rumours about the nits – that they only liked dirty hair, or greasy hair, or hair that was only washed once a week. But Jack's mum was a nurse so he knew it was all nonsense. The nits weren't fussy – as long as there was hair of a reasonable length they didn't care how clean or dirty it was.

In Jack's school the teachers tried to be really fair about the whole business and not point the finger at individuals. That was why they sent out a letter to the whole class so no one felt victimised. However, when Jack had returned to school after the summer holidays the Head had made an announcement at assembly that changed all that. He had told everyone that due to a new government initiative there was going to be school nurse in every primary school. Jack's school had been selected for a "pilot scheme" to see what benefits this new idea might have. The upshot was that a woman called Nurse Marsh would be joining the staff and she would see every child each week to check on any matters of health and fitness, including head lice. The Head had then introduced Nurse Marsh. She was an odd-looking woman with a heavily lined face that didn't move when she smiled. She told the children in assembly that she was really looking forward to making sure they were all as healthy as could be, and then her stomach rumbled loudly.

"All the kids who've been acting strangely have been to see the Nit Nurse," said Ruby as they walked down the street towards school.

Jack realised she was right. In Oscar's case for sure: he had been to see Nurse Marsh every day last week and had refused to talk about it with Jack at all. *What did she do to him?* he wondered. *Why would a Nit Nurse want to…*

Suddenly Jack stopped dead in his tracks.

"Of course!" he said, slapping

his forehead in annoyance.

"What?" said Ruby.

Jack was nodding to himself now. "I *knew* there was something strange about her face."

"Well, she is old and ugly," agreed Ruby.

"No, no, no..." replied Jack.

"Come off it," insisted Ruby. "She's got a face like a block of granite. She's not only been touched by the Ugly Stick, she's been beaten around the head by it until she's dizzy. She's a total minger."

"Yes, yes, yes, I'm not arguing with that," explained Jack. "But that's not the point I was trying to make. It's the skin on her face I was talking about. It doesn't move right. It's not natural. It's like… like she's had plastic surgery or something."

"Why would you have a face-lift and *ask* to look like that?" wondered Ruby.

"Because it's not a face-lift," said Jack with certainty. "It's a mask. She must be another GUNK Alien in disguise."

Ruby stared at him. "You're not serious."

"I am."

"The Nit Nurse is an alien?"

"I'm afraid so," said Jack.

"So what do you think she's doing to the kids?" Ruby asked.

"I don't know," Jack confessed. "But I'm going to find out. Somehow kids who

get their nits treated are losing their get-up-and-go."

"So we're looking for an alien that makes people lose interest in things," mused Ruby. "Maybe Snivel can come up with an answer."

Snivel couldn't come to school – his unusual appearance would lead to too many questions. So Jack had to wait until all his lessons were over to investigate further. As usual, Snivel arranged to meet Jack at the local park. Oscar had shown no interest in the whole situation and had decided to go home straight after school, and Ruby's mother had insisted on picking her up in the car to go and buy some new ballet shoes, so Jack was all alone. It felt weird to be on the verge of another adventure and not have his two companions by his side. At least Snivel was still there.

Except he wasn't!

When Jack reached the bench which was their usual meeting point, Snivel was nowhere to be seen. Jack sat down heavily and sighed.

A moment or two later Snivel came tearing out of some bushes and bounded up to Jack.

"Sorry," he said quickly, seeing Jack's expression. "I thought I saw that robot squirrel of Bob's..."

Jack sat up. Both Bobs – the original GUNGE contact now known as Bad Bob, and New Bob – had used a robot squirrel as a surveillance device.

"And did you?" he asked.

Snivel shook his head. "Sorry," he reported. "It was just a squirrel. So I chased it for appearance's sake."

Jack started to tell Snivel about the Nit Nurse and his suspicions about her alien nature. Snivel nodded. "I'll look it up." Before Bad Bob had made his base disappear, Snivel had managed to download the complete GUNGE alien intelligence database. He accessed the database now and within a few moments he had an answer for Jack.

"There's one alien who totally fits the bill," he announced. "It's called the Sonomarshillian."

Jack jumped up. "That sounds likely. Sono*marshi*llian – Nurse Marsh. So what can you tell me about it?"

Snivel started to rattle off the full data entry. "Sonomarshillian, inhabitant of a number of worlds in the Gamma Quadrant. Alien life-form that eats anything, but is particularly fond of small insects, such as fleas and head lice. The saliva of the Sonomarshillian contains an enzyme which has a marked soporific effect on most mammals. Creatures that are licked by the Sonomarshillian will become lethargic and lifeless. Repeated exposure to the enzyme in Sonomarshillian saliva can be fatal."

Jack paced up and down in front of Snivel. "That's got to be it. That completely fits what's happening here. She must be licking up the nits from kids' heads and leaving them... dozy."

"Lethargic," said Snivel.

"Yeah, that too," said Jack.

Snivel jumped up and started pacing alongside his master. "She'll be looking to find the GUNGE base and rescue her friends," he pointed out.

"In that case maybe we can follow her and get it back. But first I have to have proof that she *is* a Sonomarshillian. All the evidence points that way, but I have to make sure. I don't want to waste time following a Nit Nurse who just happens to be ugly."

"So what will you do?" wondered Snivel.

Jack looked grimfaced. "The only thing I can do. Go undercover. Snivel... I need to get nits."

CHAPTER THREE

The next day Jack put his plan into action.
At registration he reported to his teacher
that he had spent the whole night with an
itchy head and that he feared that he might
have nits.

"Didn't your mum have a look?" asked
Miss Cox, staring at his head
suspiciously.

"She did, but she couldn't

see anything," replied Jack. "You can have a look if you want." He thrust his head closer to his teacher, who recoiled rapidly, holding her hands out in front of her.

"No, no," she insisted, "that won't be necessary. We'll get you checked over by the expert. I'll make you an appointment with Nurse Marsh this morning."

Jack returned to his desk with a big grin on his face. The plan was working. Most of the children on his table were horrified and made silly remarks, but Jack just ignored them. He was more concerned about Oscar and Rahul, both of whom were slumped at the table looking as if they were about to fall asleep. As he looked around the classroom, Jack saw that there was at least one kid on every table in a similar state. He needed to get on with this mission fast!

Later that morning Jack was summoned to the medical room where Nurse Marsh held her nit surgery. He joined the small line of children who were due to see her. Most of the kids in front of him were in the state of semi-consciousness that Jack recognised from Oscar. One by one they were called in to see the Nurse, and each one, when they emerged, seemed even more lifeless than before. Finally it was Jack's turn.

Inside the medical room a special examination table had been installed. It was a bit like a standard medical table, but designed so that you lay on your stomach with your face through a cushioned hole cut into the surface. Once in position, the top of your head could be easily examined with the powerful Anglepoise lamp fixed to the table, but the patient was unable to see anything that was going on...

Jack's examination was brief. He had gambled that Nurse Marsh wouldn't waste time licking his head if there was no sign of nits and he was confident that he didn't have any. Luckily Nurse Marsh seemed to agree.

"You're nit free," she announced, unable to keep a slight note of disappointment out of her voice. "I'll just make a note on your record and then you can get back to class."

She turned to type something into her computer and Jack took his opportunity. Jumping down from the examination table, he quickly pulled a small object out from his pocket and looked for a suitable hiding place. *Of course – the arm of the Anglepoise lamp!* Keeping one eye on the mysterious

nurse, Jack fixed the tiny video camera to the arm of the lamp. With its wide-angle lens it would give a good view of anything the lamp was pointed at. The signal would be picked up by a receiver in Jack's locker. Nurse Marsh finished at the computer and turned around.

"Off you go then."

Jack didn't need to be told twice.

But Jack didn't go directly back to his classroom. Instead he went to his locker and collected the rest of his equipment and then disappeared to the old boys' toilets. Over the summer the children's toilets at one end of the school had been refurbished and a flash new automatic washbasin had been installed. Now no one used the old toilets unless they were absolutely desperate, which meant that they spent most of the day the place was completely empty, and that suited Jack just fine.

Jack entered the toilets and found that, as expected, no one else was there. He slipped into a cubicle, locked the door and put down the toilet seat so he could sit down. *So far, so good*, he thought. Opening his backpack, he pulled out his video receiver and his hand-held gaming machine. Jack had developed a way to feed a video signal into the hand-held, using the small screen as a TV screen. He activated the device and a moment later the screen flickered into life. The image was crystal clear. Another child was now in the medical room with the Nit Nurse and Jack watched, fascinated, as the boy laid down on the table and put his face into the cushioned hole. The nurse began to examine his hair. First, she used her hands. Moving with amazing speed her fingers closed on something moving in the boy's hair. Holding the tiny insect up between finger and thumb, she dropped it into her mouth.

Ew! That's just gross, thought Jack.

But it was only the beginning. Now a long forked tongue emerged from the

nurse's mouth. It was like a tentacle, at least a metre long and dripping with thick white saliva. Jack's stomach turned as the tongue began to move through the boy's hair, collected nits as it went. The tongue moved faster and faster as the alien became more and more excited about the tasty treats she was finding. The image on Jack's screen wobbled and then it was falling. The camera must have become dislodged. The image went all fuzzy for a moment before coming back into focus. Jack found himself looking directly into Nurse Marsh's eyes.

Oh, no!

Jack dropped the hand held console and grabbed his bag. He knew the video signal only went one way – Nurse Marsh couldn't possibly have seen him. But despite himself he was still terrified. He flung open the door of the cubicle and skidded across the tiles to the main door. Jack opened it, hurtled out into the corridor and began running. He scuttled around a corner and came to an abrupt stop. Nurse Marsh was coming in the opposite direction. Without waiting to see if she had seen him, Jack reversed his direction and went rapidly back the way he had just come.

Then he realised with horror that he was at a dead end. The stairs at this end of the building had been blocked off years ago and were used for storage of old papers and files. There was no way out. The only rooms down here that were used were the toilets – and that hardly every happened. Taking a gamble that they would be as empty as the boys', Jack pushed open the door to the girls' toilets. Inside there was a long row of cubicles. Jack quickly entered one and put the seat down. He sat on it and pulled his feet up so they couldn't be seen under the gap in the door, then tried to calm his breathing down. His heart was beating so hard and fast he was scared that it would give him away on its own.

For a long moment nothing happened. *Has she taken the bait?* he thought. *Has she gone into the boys' toilets and found them deserted?*

Suddenly he heard a loud bang as the main door opened. Someone came into the toilets. Jack almost stopped breathing. One by one the cubicle doors slammed open with a hollow *boom*. Finally the door of Jack's cubicle rattled. But the lock held. Jack prepared himself. He would only have one shot at this. A shadow fell across the floor of the cubicle as the person outside got

down on their knees. Any moment now a
face would appear in the gap between the
door and the floor. Jack grabbed the top of
the partition walls with both hands and
swung himself forward, kicking out with
both legs. SMASH! The lock gave way and
the door exploded out into the room,

knocking the kneeling Nurse Marsh over.
Jack continued his momentum and, stepping
as lightly as possible on the now prone
door, he jumped over the alien and ran out
of the toilets without looking back.

Heart pumping, he hurried back to his
classroom.

Are you all right Jack?" enquired Miss
Cox, seeing the state he was in.

"I, er, got a bit flustered in the
medical room," Jack explained
hurriedly, "but I'm OK now." *I hope,*
he added in his head.

Back in the old girls' loos Nurse
Marsh pushed the cubicle door off
of her and got to her feet. Her
mask/face was as impossible to
read as ever, but behind it her alien

eyes were burning with anger. She was going to have to teach someone a lesson about what happened to people who cross a Sonomarshillian. All she had to do was work out which human child had dared to spy on her. She reached into her pocket and pulled out the hand-held console the spy had been using. She had found it in the boys' toilets. With this evidence it wouldn't take her long to find the culprit.

And then they would pay.

cHAPTER FOUR

When Jack got home there was a squirrel waiting for him in the tree house. It was sitting on the porch of the shed, arms folded and tapping one foot on the floor impatiently. Seeing the squirrel, Jack hurried up the ladder.

"Have you been waiting long?" he asked as he opened the tree house door and let

the squirrel inside. Without answering immediately the squirrel jumped up on to Jack's workbench so it could look Jack in the eye.

"A couple of hours," said a female voice from somewhere inside the squirrel. "But that's not important right now. I need to talk to you about the future of GUNGE."

The squirrel was, of course, the surveillance robot that Bad Bob had used in the past. Now it was just about the only bit of alien technology that New Bob had at her disposal; all the rest of GUNGE's arsenal of alien weapons and devices was in the missing base.

Jack sat down in one of the beanbags.

"I'm really glad you got in touch," he began. "There's something I need to talk to you about."

The Squirrel-Bot shook its head. "It will

have to wait. The most important thing is that we have to find the base and get it back in the next couple of days – if we don't they are going to close GUNGE down!"

"What?" Jack was shocked. How could the government close down GUNGE at a time like this when aliens were queuing up to invade planet Earth?

"There are lots of people in the Establishment who don't have a lot of time for GUNGE. They think it's a waste of money and a bit of a joke. Most people in government don't think aliens even exist," explained New Bob. "If we can get back the base – and the aliens you've already captured – then they will have to believe us. If we don't, then the GUNK Aliens will win and we'll all end up as snot cows, drained of every last drop of mucus to supply energy for the alien alliance."

"Oh," said Jack. "We'd better find the base then."

"Yes indeed," said New Bob.

"There must be some way to track it down with technology," Jack suggested. "The energy signal from that place must be enormous."

"But it's shielded," replied New Bob. "The only way to track that kind of shielded energy signature would be with a powerful alien subwave tracker."

"I don't suppose we've got one of those?" asked Jack, hopefully.

"We've got three," announced New Bob proudly. "But they are all inside the base."

Jack's heart sank. "Oh," he said. "So the thing we need to find the missing base is inside the missing base. It's a bit like when Mum shut her car keys inside the car."

"Except in that case she knew where her car was," New Bob pointed out. "So all she had to do was get the nice AA man to come and help her."

"How do you know that?" said Jack.

"Well… um… That's what people do, isn't it?" said New Bob. "When they lose their car keys? They call the AA."

"I guess," said Jack, only half-convinced. But then he

had another thought. He leapt to his feet. "You said you had three of these subwave things, yeah? So where did you get them all?"

"Salvaged from three different alien scout ships," said New Bob.

"So this tracker is standard equipment on scout ships?"

The squirrel nodded.

"So all we have to do is find another scout ship."

The squirrel was shaking its head again. "We're going round in circles. How are we going to find a scout ship without the tracker?"

Jack grinned. He had had an idea.

Zana Perkins was not a happy lady. The pretty blonde-haired TV presenter, once the host of *Animal Ark* and *Zoo Watch Live*

Update, had not been having a very good time recently. Her career, which had been going along quite happily, had hit a brick wall and now things were going from bad to worse. Currently she was walking – or, more precisely, wading – through foul-smelling sludge, on a farm in the middle of nowhere. She was trying to think of it as sludge but she knew what it really was. Animal poo and rotting vegetation. The farm seemed to have it everywhere and now Zana did too.

"So you'll be back with your camera crew this afternoon?" the farmer was saying to her. He was a cheerful red-faced man who looked like he was made out of a lot of over-inflated misshapen balls. His clothes, which may once have been a red and black checked shirt and a pair of jeans, were so coated with layers of dried mud and muck that it was hard to see that he had any on at all. A mucky hand reached out to her and reluctantly she took it with the lightest of touches, and allowed him to shake her hand before quickly snatching it back. She tried not to gag as she wiped some brown and foul-smelling liquid from her hand on her jacket.

"Oh, yes," she said, trying to ignore the awful stench all around her. "We'll be back and we'll get a great little feature about your new muck-powered generator for the local news."

Zana squelched her way back towards her car. When she got back to the office she'd have a few words to say to her editor. He'd completely failed to explain the nature of the location of this "incredible green power generator" that she was to cover. She was wearing quite the wrong outfit, including her new shoes, which were now

totally ruined. At least the high heels were keeping her feet above the sludge – well, the back of her feet. Her toes, however, were wet and filthy – she could feel something squishy and cold between them and could bear it no longer. She leant against the car, removed her shoe and tried to flick the wodge of semi-solid stinky brown material out from between her toes. Whatever it was (and she really, really didn't want to know) it was a bit like modelling clay and didn't want to move.

She tried again, flicking harder, and suddenly lost balance. Unable to find anything to hold on to she fell slowly backwards.

SPLAT!

The brown sludge broke her fall, but the impact threw a shower of the material into the air, coating her beautiful car. Zana lay there for a moment, utterly miserable, as the foul wetness seeped slowly into her clothes, up her skirt and down her neck.

Zana sighed. If only she had managed to get to the bottom of the alien story. Four times she'd encountered the same trio of kids and their slightly odd-looking dog. Four times they had nearly led her to uncovering evidence of alien activity on planet earth. But each and every time something had prevented her from holding on to the evidence. *If only I had, maybe I wouldn't be lying in foul-smelling sludge for a living,* she thought. Zana made herself a promise. If she ever saw those kids again she would stop at nothing to get the alien story.

No matter what it took.

Jack was being very brave. Going back to school after the incident with Nurse Marsh took a lot of courage. He wished he had his friends with him, but Ruby had been out and Oscar had been asleep so he only had Snivel for company.

Jack knew that there was a CCTV camera pointing at the main gate, connected to monitors in the School Office – which was uncomfortably close to Nurse Marsh's room – so he went directly to the secret entrance. Part of the school's playing field ran alongside the park and a couple of loose railings, known to a select few, allowed you to get through the fence. Jack squeezed through and then held the railings apart to allow Snivel to follow him. They began to move along the fence, keeping an eye on the school buildings the whole time. Their target was the staff car park, at the side of the school, close to the main entrance.

Jack made it his business to know which cars belonged to which teachers. When a teacher was ill or late, he was the first to know, and his early reports that a certain class could expect a supply teacher were very popular. The Nit Nurse drove a small red mini and, as he had hoped, it was one of the four cars still in the car park.

Jack turned to Snivel. "Are you sure you're happy to do this? It could be dangerous."

Snivel tried to shrug, which caused his third eye to fly open. He managed to close the eye, but then PARP – he farted. Jack gagged. He had thought he had got used to the disgusting odours given off by Snivel's on-board snot-powered generator, but this was worse than the usual.

"It's OK to be scared," he said sympathetically.

"I'm not scared," insisted Snivel. "I was just generating some extra power for my defence systems. You don't have any spare snot at the moment, do you?"

Jack sighed, then rammed a finger up his nose and had a quick rummage. He pulled it out and offered the big fat bogey he had found to Snivel, who sucked it up gratefully.

"Now I'm ready for anything," announced the robot dog and, using a power beam from his third eye, he opened the boot of the mini and jumped in. "Wish me luck."

"Just be careful," Jack said, before slamming the boot shut and hurrying off. Reaching a safe place to keep watch, he crouched down and was shocked to see that Nurse Marsh was already coming out of the school. She climbed into the mini and drove away. As the little car disappeared around a corner Jack swallowed hard.

Would he ever see Snivel again?

CHAPTER FIVE

Watching Snivel being driven off by an alien was the most depressing thing Jack had ever seen. Feeling miserable, he hurried home to the tree house to wait for word from the Snot-Bot.

In a terrible mood he mooched around, fiddling with half-finished projects without any real interest. It was no good. Without Oscar, the tree house was just a garden shed in an unusual position. For the hundredth time since getting home Jack sighed heavily. There had to be something he could do while waiting.

He called round at Oscar's house again, but Oscar's mum just told him that Oscar was too tired to come and play. So he went to Ruby's, but her mum told him that she was at ballet class.

"Oh, right," Jack said. "Ballet class, of course." He hoped he sounded like he believed her. There was no way Ruby was *really* at ballet class. She was probably climbing, or pot-holing, or something. He decided to check out the park – maybe she was doing something wild on the skateboard tubes.

There were some kids at the park, but no one had seen Ruby.

Disappointed, Jack left the park

and wandered back down the High Street. As he passed the community hall he heard some plinky plonky piano music and the unmistakable sound of dancing feet on a shiny floor. Jack couldn't help but grin to himself at the thought of Ruby actually going to a ballet lesson. *As if that would ever happen.*

"No, no, no, Ruby. Do try not to take out Elspeth with your foot when you stretch it."

The voice was posh and female and came floating out of the windows of the hall. Jack froze. *Were his ears playing tricks on him?*

"That's much better, Ruby, well done."

Jack's mouth was hanging open in complete disbelief. A fly flew in and he spat it out, disgusted. He turned round and walked into the hall. Inside there were

about a dozen girls and there, at the end of
the line, was Ruby.

Ruby, at a ballet class, wearing a tutu!

A little while later Jack and
Ruby were walking home. An
awkward silence hung

between them and both were red-faced
with embarrassment.

"This is where we need Oscar with us to
say something stupid," Jack said eventually.

"Like, 'why was that rock-climbing class
all wearing tutus?' suggested Ruby with a
hint of a smile on her face.

"Yeah, or, 'how come the karate club
were listening to someone playing a piano
during their practice?'" said Jack.

Now they were both smiling.

"I'm sorry I lied to you," said Ruby, looking
straight ahead and avoiding Jack's gaze.

Jack shrugged. "It's all right."

"No, it isn't. You shouldn't have secrets
from friends," insisted Ruby. "The thing is, I
can't lie to Mum all the time. So I've started
to *really* go to ballet. I'm still doing all the
other things, but I thought I should do just
one thing she wants."

"It looks tough," said Jack kindly.

"It is! You wouldn't believe it. First week I went I had aches in muscles I didn't know I had!" exclaimed Ruby. "Will you tell Oscar?" she added.

"Not much point at the moment is there? It's not like he's going to care. We've got to stop the Sonomarshillian and find a cure for him."

"The Sono-what?" asked Ruby.

Quickly Jack brought Ruby up to speed. He told her all about his close encounter with the Nit Nurse and who she really was. He told her about New Bob getting in contact and how GUNGE itself was under threat. And then he told her about Snivel's brave spy mission. Ruby was horrified.

"You let Snivel go off with the alien... on his own?" she said.

"It was the only way," insisted Jack. "We have to find her space ship and use the technology in it to find Bad Bob's base before it's too late."

At least this time I'm dressed in the right gear, Zana thought to herself. She was back in the brown sludge at the farm, but now she was wearing wellington boots and a thick plastic-coated pair of overalls. The interview with the farmer about his revolutionary electricity generator that used muck as a fuel had been every bit as boring to record as Zana had expected. The farmer seemed to think that muck was fascinating, but Zana couldn't see the appeal herself.

"Would you like to see the slurry pits?" asked the farmer, in the same tone of voice

as a parent offering an extra treat at the
end of a great day out.

"The what-pits?" asked Zana.

"Where we dump all the animal
excrement and let it fester," the
farmer told her with a big
smile. "We chuck just about

71

anything in there and it breaks down into a really rich and potent liquid. Smells a bit, but you get used to it."

Before Zana could think of an excuse to avoid the slurry pit part of the tour they were interrupted by the arrival of a red Mini. A strange-looking woman in a nurse's uniform got out of the car and waved at the farmer cheerily.

"My tenant," explained the farmer. "I rent out a caravan on Lower Field," he continued. "Well, I like to, but to be honest I don't get many takers. Townies don't like the smell for some reason. Nurse Marsh there doesn't seem to mind though."

Zana found herself watching the nurse quite carefully, without really knowing why. There was something about her, something odd. The nurse opened up the boot and picked up something that looked familiar to

Zana. She crossed the yard to take a closer look.

"Interesting looking dog," said Zana as she approached.

The nurse whirled round quickly with the creature in her hands. It was lying limp and rather lifeless, but nevertheless Zana recognised it immediately. It was the dog that hung around with the alien-chasing kids!

"Yes. I found it lying by the road. I don't think the poor thing is very well," the nurse was saying to her, with a fixed smile on her face that didn't spread to her eyes.

"Are you a vet as well as a nurse?" asked Zana.

"No, of course not, but I thought I might see if there was anything I could do for him," said the nurse.

Zana thought quickly. "Well, it must be his lucky day. My brother is a vet and I'm just going back to town now. Why don't I take him there?"

The Nurse frowned. "Oh, there's no need to put yourself to any bother..."

To Zana's relief the farmer had joined them. He peered at the dog. "Safest thing for a sick animal is a vet, Nurse Marsh. Let the girl take the dog. I'm sure it'll be for the best," he suggested.

The nurse looked at the farmer and then back at the limp dog in her arms, and finally nodded. She handed the dog over to Zana.

"I do hope your brother can help him," she said, but it sounded just a little forced.

A few moments later Zana was driving out of the farm with the little Snot-Bot safely on her passenger seat and a huge grin on her face. Now she might finally get some answers...

Ruby and Jack were still walking down the High Street, looking into shop windows as they chatted.

"How is Snivel going to contact you?" asked Ruby.

Jack shrugged. "I'm not sure," he confessed. "He just said he'd find a way. Like Bob does."

"Like that, you mean," said Ruby, jabbing a finger in the direction of a TV shop they were passing.

"What?" asked Jack. All he could see were loads and loads of TV screens all showing reruns of *Animal Ark*.

"There," said Ruby, pointing a little lower in the window. There, underneath the TVs, was an electronic message board. Red letters spelling out advertising messages, new prices and special offers were moving slowly left to right across the board, looping round and round again and again. Except it wasn't just advertising messages. There was also something else...

"**Jack. Snivel located. Buttercup Farm. Little Hodgekins. Bob**," read Ruby as the letters moved slowly across the panel and then reappeared at the far end.

"Little Hodgekins is a village out on the

way to the coast," said Jack. "We went through it when we were on our shark hunt."

"Then what are we waiting for?" said Ruby. "We've got a rescue mission to perform!"

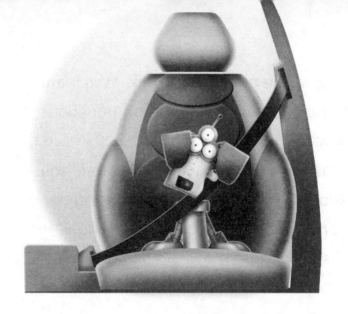

CHAPTER SIX

Zana was frustrated. As soon as she was a safe distance from the farm she had pulled over and tried to get some sense out of the dog.

"I know you can understand me," she said. "So why don't you just answer my questions?"

But the dog had just sat unmoving on the passenger seat where she had placed him. Zana began to get worried. *What if it's ill?*

she wondered. Actually, she was fairly certain that it wasn't a real dog but some kind of robot. Could robots get ill? Maybe it was just broken. Maybe the nurse had broken it. Maybe it was hungry. *Does a robot dog need food?* Zana decided to see if she could find something for it to eat. She drove on down the road and into the tiny village of Little Hodgekins.

There wasn't much in the village: a pub, a war memorial, a village green and a single shop which was part newsagent and part mini-mart. A few moments later Zana came out of the shop with a small bag containing a variety of foods and treats. As she walked back towards the car she saw two familiar children whizz past her on bikes. It was two of the alien-chasing kids! The girl and the odd-looking boy who usually had the dog with him. Zana watched as the two children rode off in the direction of Buttercup Farm. *It can't be a coincidence*, she decided. Her instincts had been right. That farmer or that nurse, one or the other of them, must be an alien in disguise. She had been right on top of the story she'd been looking for all these months and she'd nearly missed it! The camera crew had been dismissed, but Zana knew she had to go back right away and get whatever evidence she could. This time she was *not* going to miss her chance.

When Zana got back to her car she was in for another shock.

The dog had gone.

Did the children rescue it? No, it wasn't possible. How would they have known where to look? The only explanation was that the robot dog had recovered from whatever had paralysed it and made its own escape. For all Zana knew it was on its way back to the farm. Zana started up the car and threw it into a swift three-point turn.

Jack and Ruby rode past the farm entrance, taking the opportunity to have a quick glance into the farmyard as they did. Both of them spotted the Nit Nurse's red mini, but there was no sign of any people. A little bit further down the lane Jack pulled up. Quickly the two children hid their bikes in the undergrowth and looked for a way to get on to the farm. They didn't have to look very far. There was a public footpath that crossed the farm's fields. Keeping low, so as not to be seen, Jack and Ruby skulked along the footpath until they were close to the farm buildings. Then they branched off the path across the fields and towards the nearest shed.

"What's that smell?" wondered Ruby.

"I'm not sure," answered Jack. "I can't quite put my finger on it."

SQUELCH!

"I think you've put your foot in it though," said Ruby, laughing.

Jack looked down and saw that he had just stepped into a very large, wet and smelly cowpat. "Oh, gross," he muttered, pulling his foot out and seeing how filthy his trainer was.

"Watch your step," said Ruby, trying to stop her giggling.

"It's not funny, you know," complained Jack.

"Sorry," said Ruby. Or at least that's what she *tried* to say. What she *actually* said was closer to "So—*aaaaaaaaaargh*", a startled scream which ended in a thick SPLURGE sound.

Jack spun round, but there was no sign of Ruby. He took a step closer to where she had last been standing and realised that he was on the lip of a giant hole. Cautiously he looked over the edge and saw that Ruby was

about two metres below him, up to her neck in a thick brown substance that gave off such an obnoxious stench it made the cow poo on his foot smell like expensive perfume.

"Don't just stand there, help me!" cried Ruby. Jack could see that the liquid was

pulling her under, like foul-smelling
quicksand. He had to act quickly. He pulled
off his rucksack and began rifling through it
for something he could use.

"Jack, hurry, I'm going
under," shouted Ruby, and Jack
was shocked to hear the fear

in her voice. This was a girl who thought nothing of performing jumps on a jet ski. At the bottom of the bag he finally found what he was looking for – some thin but strong rope.

"Don't worry, I came prepared," he told Ruby happily. "Catch the end of this." He threw one end of the rope down into the pit.

"Got it," said Ruby.

"Right, hold on," Jack replied. He started to pull on the rope. He felt it take the strain as it was pulled taut and then it began to move. He could feel Ruby's weight as she was pulled free of the slurry. Then disaster – his foot slipped. Then his other trainer lost its footing. Suddenly it was Jack who was moving, sliding ever closer to the lip of the slurry pit. The rescue was going completely wrong.

Just then, Jack felt someone grab his belt and yank him backwards. Moments later an arm snaked round his waist and pulled him to his feet. Together the mysterious stranger and Jack were able to regain the lost ground. Centimetre by centimetre they moved back from the pit edge, pulling at the rope. With each step they seemed to get on to harder, firmer ground. Finally the bedraggled figure of Ruby appeared over the rim of the pit. Although covered with disgusting slurry she managed to grin and, with some of her usual character intact, she waved a cheery hand at Jack.

"Great fun, but I don't fancy doing it again!" she joked.

As Jack dropped the rope, he turned round to see who had helped them. His jaw dropped.

"You?

Zana smiled at them both. "Yes, me. And this time I'm not going anywhere until you tell me everything you know about the aliens."

CHAPTER SEVEN

Something very fast was moving along the main A345 between Little Hodgekins and the city. Some people thought it was a wild fox or hare dashing along the road, others thought it might be a tiny remote-controlled motorbike, and some just felt the rush of air as something zipped past them.

Whatever it was, it didn't

stop for red lights, or pause at junctions. With relentless determination the speeding object just moved. Very fast.

Snot-Bots are remarkable creatures. Originally developed by the master engineers of Vewyrn Minor, they were designed to locate and capture potential sources of snot. Snivel had been captured and reprogrammed by some of the best brains on the planet but, when push came to shove, he was still a Snot-Bot and there wasn't a creature born on Earth, nor vehicle made on Earth, that could move faster than a Snot-Bot in Ultimate Speed Mode.

By the time he reached Jack's house Snivel was glowing and giving off enough heat to cook school dinners for a week. Pausing only to use the garden sprinkler to cool down his outer shell, Snivel hurried to the tree house, but quickly determined that

Jack wasn't there. He hacked into the mobile phone network and tried calling Ruby. There was no reply. Finally the robot dog considered his options. No Jack. No Ruby. There was only one other human he could try – the stupid one.

"Come on, I just saved your lives. Give me a break, can't you?" Zana pleaded with the children.

"It's best you don't know," insisted Jack. "For your own safety."

"I can handle myself," replied Zana. "And anyway, don't the public deserve to know what's going on? How do you think your parents would react if they knew you were keeping this all secret?"

Jack shrugged. "If I told my mum there was a good reason

for it, then she'd trust me."

Zana turned to Ruby. "What about your mum?"

"My mum?" said Ruby. "She'd totally freak out. She gets worried if I'm five minutes late getting the newspaper from the corner shop. There's no way she could cope with all this! Look, you have to believe us – some stories are best left untold."

Zana looked at them both and then shook her head firmly. "You're wrong," she stated confidently. "And I'm going to show you why."

Oscar groaned and yawned. "Gerrof!" he muttered, pushing away whatever it was that was standing on his chest.

Snivel held his ground.

"Wake up," he barked.

"What?" said Oscar, managing to open his eyes this time.

"You've got to wake up," insisted the Snot-Bot, sitting on the boy's chest and poking his face with one paw. "Jack needs you."

Oscar struggled to sit up, forcing Snivel to step to one side.

"Jack needs me?" he repeated.

"Yes, Jack needs you to have a shower."

"What?"

"A shower. You know: you get naked, pour hot water on yourself, use soap and shampoo to get clean..."

Oscar sniffed. "I know what a shower is. I have one every week."

"Every *week*?!"

Oscar shrugged. "Well, I don't want to waste water do I? Is it Tuesday then? I have my shower on Tuesdays usually."

"Yes," said Snivel. "Yes, it's Tuesday. So go and have your shower and make sure you wash your hair."

Zana had found a large cowshed at the back of the farm buildings that seemed different to the rest. It was a big structure, one that should have accommodated lots of cows. But there was no animal smell coming from within. If anything the smell from inside was factory-like –metallic and clean. And to go with the smell there was a faint hum, like a very efficient electrical generator.

This is it, Zana thought to herself. She got her camera out of her bag and switched it on, ready to capture the evidence of alien activity that she had been looking for all this time. Carefully she slid open the massive doors of the cow shed. Inside it was dark and it took a moment for her eyes to adjust. There was some kind of structure in the centre of the shed. Metallic and shiny...

Oh, wow, thought Zana.

It was a spaceship. A real-life spaceship.

Zana gasped as she took in the details. The scars and impact marks of space debris

and meteorites. She had seen similar things on NASA's space shuttle, but this was different. This looked like it had travelled much further through space. It was truly alien.

Zana quickly took some photographs. Each shot was going to be worth a fortune. Unable to contain her curiosity she took a step closer to the spaceship and then

another. Finally she reached out a hand to touch the surface of the machine. To think she was about to touch something truly alien! Carefully, almost lovingly, she let her fingers caress the smooth metal.

EEEOOOEEOOOEEE!

A shrill siren sounded and massive arc lamps switched on, flooding the room with white light. Zana threw up her hands to

shield her eyes, but it was too late – she was temporarily blinded by the light.

"Quick, this way!" said a voice.

It was Jack. He and Ruby had followed the journalist and were now ready to try and repay the favour for rescuing them earlier. Each of them grabbed one of the woman's hands and together they led her back towards the door. The three of them stumbled out into the outside world and stopped dead.

They were in a narrow passageway formed by two further barns. In front of them, arranged in a semi circle, were the five aliens that they had captured before: the Squillibloat, the Burrapong, the Flartibug, the Slurrisnoat and the Grackle-Shaffler. Just beyond the aliens they could see the disgusting slurry pit Ruby had fallen into.

The door behind them slammed shut and when they turned they found that their only escape route had been cut off by the thing

known as "Nurse Marsh". As they watched, she pulled the human face mask away from her head to reveal the glutinous blob that was the natural form of the Sonomarshillian. Its long sticky tongue slipped out of its monstrous mouth and flicked wads of thick salvia into the air.

"To paraphrase your own silly slogan... Activate Jack Trap!" it announced, and then all of the aliens began to laugh.

cHAPTER EIGHT

Oscar stumbled out of the shower, more awake than he had been for weeks, rubbing himself dry with a massive towel.

"It isn't Tuesday at all," he complained.

"No, but it was important that you showered," Snivel told him. While Oscar finished drying himself and got dressed, Snivel filled him in on everything that had been happening. "So the upshot is I don't know where Ruby and Jack are," he confessed, concluding his story.

"I do," said Oscar brightly pulling his mobile out of his pocket. "Ruby texted me earlier, but I still had that alien saliva gunk on my head and I wasn't really bothered." Oscar showed the text message to Snivel. "Gone to Bluebell Farm, Little Hodgekins."

Snivel started to shake. "Oh, no. They're both in terrible danger. There's only one person who can help us. Come on." Snivel dashed out of the room and Oscar hurried to follow him.

Back at the farm the GUNK Aliens were enjoying their moment of triumph. In truth they were probably overdoing it. Every few seconds one of them would start cackling wildly and before you knew it they were all at it. Eventually their laughing would subside and they would begin to talk normally, and then one of them would start to giggle and the whole thing would begin all over again.

Zana sighed. Her eyesight had recovered, but she was not sure that was a good thing. The six slightly hysterical aliens surrounding her was a sight she could have done without.

"What do you want with us?" she asked the aliens as their laughter began to fade away for the eighth or ninth time.

"With you – nothing," the Sonomarshillian told her. "We just wanted the boy. We've got a nice cell waiting for him in our friend Bob's base."

"Bad Bob's base is here?" Jack asked.

The alien nodded, making its jelly-like head wobble madly. "The farmer's caravan," it told him. "Bob's in there now, making things ready for you."

Ruby grabbed Jack's hand and gave it a squeeze. He shot her a quick look and managed to smile.

"For you, Jack Brady," continued the Sonomarshillian, "this is the end of the line."

Oscar couldn't believe it. Snivel had taken him to *Ruby's* house. But Ruby was at the farm. What use could it possibly be to go to her house? There was no one there except her mum. "Are you sure?" said Oscar.

Snivel sighed. "Just ring the doorbell. I'd do it myself only I can't reach."

Oscar shrugged and rang the doorbell. He didn't know what he was meant to say to Ruby's mum. Luckily Snivel made the decision for him.

The door opened and Ruby's mum stood there looking at Oscar and Snivel.

"Hello boys," she said brightly. "What can I do for you?"

"Sorry," said Snivel, "but I need to talk to Bob."

"Bob doesn't live here, you idiot, Ruby does. And so does her mum," said Oscar.

"And so does Bob," said Ruby's mum. "*I'm* Bob. The New Bob anyway. So what's happening?"

Oscar stared, open-mouthed.

"*Trouble* is what's happening," said Snivel, "Big trouble."

The journey down the A345 was a blur for Oscar. Partly because Ruby's mum's sports car seemed capable of travelling at somewhere around the speed of sound, but mostly because he had to get his head around the fact that Ruby's mum – Ruby's over-protective, never-let-her-daughter-do-anything-dangerous mum – was a GUNGE agent.

"I've always let my family believe I was a secretary in a boring government department," Ruby's mum explained as she hand-braked turned round a sharp bend. "It was simpler and safer for everyone."

"So if you're a secret agent, why do you refuse to let Ruby do anything even remotely exciting?" Oscar asked as the countryside whizzed past in a complete blur.

"Because I knew it was the best way to make her try every dangerous sport going," answered Ruby's mum with a grin, shifting gears as the engine roared. "She's a girl after my own heart. She's never going to do something her *mum* tells her to, is she?!"

The car roared on.

The aliens were still laughing. The whole situation was too amusing for words. For months Jack and his friends had been seeking out and trapping them, and now at last the tables had been turned.

A figure in dark glasses and a grey suit appeared in the distance approaching rapidly. It was Bob – the original Bob.

"You really aren't quite the genius everyone thinks you are Jack, are you?" he said as he joined his alien allies. He high-fived those of them who had hands and gave a thumbs up to the others.

"I sabotaged the Blower, didn't I?" said Jack proudly. The Blower was an intergalactic communicator that the aliens needed to call down their various invasion fleets.

"You only slowed things down. The aliens are coming. Earth will become a Snot Farm and I will be Life President and Chief Executive of Planet Earth Snot Incorporated," Bad Bob told the children and Zana proudly.

A hundred metres away Ruby's mum, Oscar and Snivel watched using high-powered sound, and, vision, amplifying surveillance glasses.

"He's totally mad, isn't he?" said Oscar.

"Barking," agreed Ruby's mum, a.k.a. New Bob.

"So what to we do?" wondered Oscar.

"Snivel Trap "em, of course," said Snivel.

"Can you manage all of them?" asked Ruby's mum.

"That slurry pit is full of material I can use to generate energy – not as good as snot, but good enough," Snivel told them.

"What's a slurry pit?" asked Oscar.

"You don't want to know," Ruby's mum told him.

"Trouble is," continued Snivel, "I need to get into that pit without being seen."

Oscar grinned and started rummaging in

his rucksack. He pulled out the voice-
programmable helicopter that Jack had
been working on. "How's about this?"

Jack tried not to yawn. Bad Bob was still
ranting on about how great and wonderful
things would be when he took
control of everything. Jack
couldn't help feeling that they

would only be great and wonderful for Bob.

Suddenly he felt Ruby nudging him. "Look up," she whispered.

Jack looked past Bob and the aliens into the sky above him and it was all he could do not to smile. Coming towards them, hanging under the voice-directed helicopter he had designed, was Snivel. The robot dog seemed to be heading for the slurry pit. Jack realised that Snivel was planning to drop into the pit. *I must keep the aliens from looking up*, he thought.

Jack stretched his arms out and yawned in an exaggerated and deliberate fashion.

"You do go on, don't you? It's a wonder this lot put up with you. But then these six are not exactly the top grade GUNK Aliens are you? Not even Second Division I'd say." Jack could see that the aliens were not liking what they were hearing. All eyes were on him. Snivel was almost in position. The tiny hum of the helicopter engine was just audible. Jack raised his voice.

"Actually that's rubbish, isn't it? Division Two? You're not even in the main leagues I reckon."

And now Snivel was directly above the pit. He let go of the chopper and fell. As he fell into the slurry behind the aliens he shouted, "Trap!" Then he disappeared into the brown sludge.

The aliens turned round, confused. Jack was also flummoxed. Trap? What did Snivel mean, trap? Was it a code word or…

Ah.

Jack turned to Ruby. "He wants to Snivel Trap them!" he said. "But he has to be underneath them!"

Ruby looked at the aliens in front of them, then at the

slurry pit. She grinned.

"When I say 'run', run," Jack whispered to Ruby and Zana and then, without further warning, he shouted "RUN!"

The aliens were taken completely by surprise as the two children and the journalist rushed at them. Zana went left, darting between the Squillibloat and the Burrapong. Ruby went right, speeding through the tiny gap between the Slurrisnoat and the Grackle-Shaffler. Jack ran directly at the Flartibug then side stepped at the last minute, hotly pursued by the Sonomarshillian.

Zana and Ruby danced nimbly around the lip of the

slurry pit, but Jack wasn't so good at sports. He screeched to a stop, his toes hanging over the edge of the foul-smelling hole. Very carefully he turned around to see that the aliens – all six ofthem – had him surrounded. Slowly, they began to advance.

"I guess I'm going to have to jump," shouted Jack, louder than necessary so that the aliens would hear. Luckily Oscar was also listening. Oscar ordered the chopper to repeat the flight plan.

Jack watched as his helicopter responded to Oscar's voice instructions and executed a 180-degree turn. *I need to time this just right*, he thought to himself. The chopper sped towards him, flying low over the heads of the aliens. Jack turned, flexed his knees and launched himself high into the air above the pit.

Roaring angrily the aliens leapt into space after him, tentacles and arms grasping for Jack, but Jack was no longer there. He'd managed to grab the straps that Snivel had used to hang from the chopper and was rising rapidly into the sky. At the same time, Ruby and Zana charged the

aliens from behind, knocking those that hadn't already fallen of their own accord into the slurry pit, towards the fetid mess of stinky goo and... Snivel!

Jack looked down to see that all the aliens were struggling in the disgusting slime.

"ACTIVATE SNIVEL TRAP!" he shouted from above.

There was an enormous bang and a flash, and then a large metallic box bobbed to the surface of the slurry, smoke drifting from its lid. It was Snivel in his trap mode.

The chopper lowered Jack towards the ground and he let go and landed nonchalantly next to Ruby. "Now that's Premier league alien, catching!" he said, smiling.

CHAPTER NINE

At last the team were reunited. It had taken Ruby's mum (Jack and Ruby were still finding it difficult to see her as New Bob) some time to get the captives out of the Snivel Trap, but finally the job was done. Now the aliens were safely secured within the massive vaults of the GUNGE base. Bad Bob had managed to escape, but Ruby's mum was confident that he wouldn't remain at large for long.

Back in his dog form, Snivel came bounding down the corridor to join Jack, Ruby and Oscar. The three kids were excitedly going over their adventures, trying to outdo each other in gross details.

Another figure lurked nearby – Zana. In all the excitement everyone had forgotten about her and, unnoticed by anyone, she had quietly sneaked into the base, through the door of the farmer's caravan. After all the other shocks she had been through she was not surprised that an enormous secret base was somehow hidden inside a tiny caravan. She was too excited to be surprised. At last she had her story.

Meanwhile, the children were exploring the base and had found a strange area at the end of a corridor. There were no doors or exits, making the entire corridor somewhat of a dead end. The area at the end had strange, brightly painted white walls and a peculiar shiny floor surface. A mirror-effect ceiling reflected the many lights.

"What do you think this place is?" wondered Jack.

"The GUNGE disco floor?" suggested Oscar.

They all laughed.

"How about a photo?" said Zana, suddenly stepping up on to the metallic platform from the corridor. The whole gang in their moment of triumph!"

The three children began to protest, but Zana had them cornered. She had her camera in her hand.

"Too bright in here," she muttered, looking through the view finder. "I'll just switch some of these lights off.."

She reached out for some switches on one of the walls and flicked one.

"N—" began Jack.

VAZROOOM! There was an extraordinary sound like an elephant's trumpet played backwards and a sequence of blinding flashes.

Jack, Oscar, Ruby and Zana blinked, trying to get their eyes to work.

"Oh no," said Snivel in a grave tone.

Jack's vision began to come back into focus. But something was wrong. Very, very wrong.

He was no longer standing on the ground.

He was floating.

"We're in zero-gravity," announced Snivel.

Jack took in his surroundings. All of them were still together but they were no longer in the base. The windows gave a clue. Outside there was nothing but the inky blackness of space and pinpoints of light.